Hello, Goodbye

A ZEBRA BOOK

Written by David Lloyd
Illustrated by Meg Palmer

PUBLISHED BY
WALKER BOOKS
LONDON

A tree stood quietly
in the sunshine.

Someone stepped out
and said 'Hello!'
Very loudly.

It was a bear.

Two bees flew in.
'Hello! Hello!' they said.
Very busily.

Along came a big red bird.
What did it say?
'Hello!' Very quickly.

Suddenly voices
all over the tree
were saying 'Hello!'

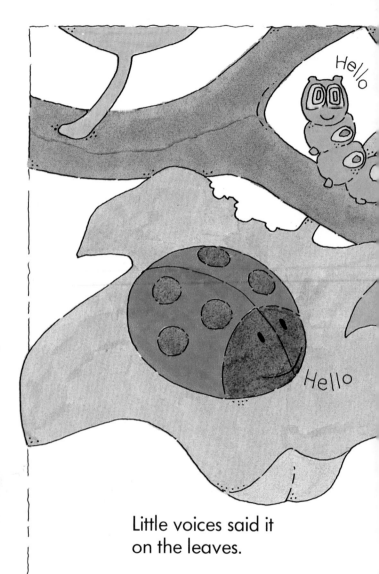

Little voices said it
on the leaves.

Squeaky voices said it
on the branches.

Deep-down voices said it among the roots.

A drop of rain fell
on the bear's nose.
Splash!

Raindrops fell all over the bear.
Splish! Splash! Splosh!

'Goodbye! Goodbye!'
said the two bees. Very busily.

'Goodbye!' said the big red bird.
Very quickly.

What did all the voices
on the tree say?
What did the bear say?
Very loudly.

The tree stood quietly again.
Everyone had gone.
'Hello rain!' it said.
Very, very quietly.